EMMETT'S PIG

HarperCollins*Publishers*

EMMETT'S PIG

BY **Mary Stolz**

❧❧

ILLUSTRATED BY

Garth Williams

WATERCOLORS BY ROSEMARY WELLS

Library of Congress Cataloging-in-Publication Data
Stolz, Mary, date
    Emmett's pig / by Mary Stolz ; illustrated by Garth Williams ;
watercolors by Rosemary Wells.
        p.   cm.
    Summary: Emmett loves pigs, but when his parents refuse to move to a
farm or let him raise a pig in their apartment, he runs out of ideas.
    ISBN 0-06-028746-2. — ISBN 0-06-028747-0 (lib. bdg.)
    [1. Pigs—Fiction.]   I. Williams, Garth, ill.   II. Rosemary Wells, ill.
III. Title.
PZ7.S875854 Em   2003   2001024750
[E]—dc21   CIP
                                                              AC

1 2 3 4 5 6 7 8 9 10
❖

For our grandchildren,
Holly and Tom Jaleski
—M.S.

Emmett was a boy who liked pigs. He liked them better than birds or fish, better than cats or dogs. He liked them better than any of the animals at the zoo. Better than lions, tigers, monkeys, camels, seals, bears, or elephants.

Better even than hippos.

Emmett had pigs in his room. He had a bank pig, and paper pigs, wooden pigs, and jigsaw puzzles about pigs. He had a pink stuffed pig with black button eyes. He had pictures of pigs and books about pigs. Sometimes he had pigs, lots of pigs, in his dreams.

But he had never seen a real live pig.

"Why are there no pigs in the zoo?" he asked his father.

"Because pigs live on farms."

"Farms are in the country, aren't they?"

"That's where they are, all right," said his father.

"Well, where *is* the country?"

"Outside the city."

"Very far from here?"

"Pretty far."

"I see," said Emmett. He added, "Can we go to the country and see a pig?"

"Someday," said his father.

Emmett sighed.

He went to his mother and said, "May I have a pig in my room?"

"No, dear, you may not have a pig in your room."

"Why can't I?"

"Because pigs live on farms, where there is a lot of grass and dirt."

"We could get some dirt and grow grass in part of my room. My pig would think it was a farm."

"Your father and I wouldn't think it was, and you may not have dirt and grass in *any* part of your room."

EXTENSION

In bed that night, Emmett had a wonderful idea.

In the morning, as they were eating breakfast, he said. "I know what let's do! Let's us go live on a farm!"

"Emmett!" said his father. "Stop this about pigs! My job is in the city, and I would not know how to be a farmer."

Emmett went to his room to think.

He could not bring a pig to live with him in the city.

He could not go to a farm where he could live with a pig.

He really did not know what to do.

He went back to his mother and father, who were still eating.

"When I grow up," he said in a loud voice, "I am going to be a farmer. I am going to have a *lot* of pigs. My special pig will be named King Emmett. He will sleep in my room with me."

"Even on a farm," said his father, "pigs don't live in bedrooms."

"Where do they live?"

"Pigs' digs are called pigpens."

"Well, that's all right. I'll sleep with him in the pigpen."

"Ah," said his father.

"We will come to visit you at your pigpen," said his mother. "Once in a while," she added.

"Cool," said Emmett.

One morning, Emmett sat up in bed. It was the thirty-first day of May, his birthday. He got presents from his two grandmothers, presents from his two grandfathers, and presents from some cousins who came to share the cake. He liked all of it very much.

He did not see anything with a tag on it saying,

Love from Mother and Dad.

"Emmett," said his father, when the presents had been opened, and the cake eaten, and the guests gone. "We are going to take you for a ride in the car."

"We'll call it your birthday ride," said his mother. "There's a present for you at the end of it."

They drove through the city.

"Is my present very far away?" asked Emmett.

"Pretty far," said his father.

They drove through a tunnel.

"Is my present sort of small?" Emmett asked.

"Pretty small," said his mother.

"Will it get bigger?"

"Oh, yes," said his father and mother together. "It will get bigger."

Emmett smiled to himself. He thought he knew what his present was going to be.

After a long time, they turned off the
highway onto a two-lane road, then onto
a dirt road, then onto a gravel driveway.
There was a farm!
And there were Mr. and Mrs. Carson,
the farmers, waiting for them.

Emmett looked all around.

He saw a garden and a barn and a silo and a pond and a meadow where cows were calmly grazing.

And then!

Then he saw a row of beautiful pigpens.
"Shall we walk over there?" asked Mr. Carson.
"Oh, yes," said Emmett. And he ran.

In one of the pigpens, there was a
big pig mother and her babies.

One of them looked very special to
Emmett.

This little pig had a small, curly tail
and round, happy eyes, and he stood
on his little hoofs, looking right up at
Emmett.

Emmett stood looking at this piglet for a long time, not speaking. Then he said, "Is that one mine?"

"He is," said his mother and father.

"Really, really mine?"

"Really yours."

"He will live here on the farm, but he will always be your pig," said his father.

"Oh, thank you, thank you! He is *just* what I wanted."

"We know that," said his mother and father together.

"His name is King Emmett," said Emmett.

"Well, well," said Mr. Carson as he lifted King Emmett out of the pen, "this is the first time we have ever had royalty living with us."

King Emmett squealed and wriggled and jumped to the grass and started running. Emmett ran after him. Past the barn and the silo, past the garden and the farmhouse they went running. They ran back and forth across the meadow. The calm cows paid them no attention.

After a long time, they stopped running and sat down. Side by side.

All afternoon, Emmett and his birthday pig played together and sat together.

When the sun was going down, Mr. Carson
put the king back with his mother and his sisters
and his brothers.

Emmett sat on a stump and looked at them.
Because they were pigs, he admired them all,
but mostly he admired the handsomest, biggest,
pinkest pig of the litter: his very own King
Emmett, who was still looking up at him.

"He knows me," said Emmett.

"Of course he does," said Mr. Carson.

It was late when Emmett and his parents got
back to the city, and Emmett went right to bed
so he could begin dreaming about King Emmett.

Now, once a month, his father and mother drive him to the farm so that he and King Emmett can spend a whole day together.

Every week, Emmett writes a letter to King Emmett, in care of Mr. Carson.

Every week, Mr. Carson writes back, giving news of the farm, and especially of the royal pig.

Now Emmett's dreams have in them one pig and one boy. They are both named Emmett, and they are very good friends.

WHEN I WAS LITTLE, there was one artist who charmed me in every book. It was Garth Williams. His was an unfailing instinct for how a character should look and exactly what moment in the text to illustrate. My respect for his artistry grew as I became an illustrator myself. I believe Garth Williams and Maurice Sendak are the two great geniuses of twentieth-century illustration in America.

Reproducing Garth Williams's preseparated two-color art in gentle color was the greatest challenge. Happily the original black-line illustrations were found in pristine condition in a vault in Texas. We reproduced them in light-gray ink on heavy Winsor & Newton handmade watercolor stock. Each drawing was then colored using the exact paints Garth had available to him in the fifites, in a palette chosen from his color work in other books.

This experience has been a labor of love for me. I welcome this opportunity, with the help of the editors and production staff at HarperCollins, to bring some of this great genius's work to a new generation of readers.

—ROSEMARY WELLS